AF266659

Who's Knocking at My Door?

Terrie Stadler

ReadersMagnet, LLC

ReadersMagnet, LLC
10620 Treena Street, Suite 230 | San Diego, California, 92131 USA
1.619.354.2643 | www.readersmagnet.com

Book design copyright © 2021 by ReadersMagnet, LLC. All rights reserved.
Cover design by Ericka Obando
Interior design by Mary Mae Romero

It was a new year and we had just moved into a great house in a rural area. Of course this was very different compared to the suburban community we had just left. Our new home had more land, a very large storage building and a small country pond. Our lives would change as we became accustomed to our new life and surroundings meeting new friends in the process.

This pond supported an array of marshy grasses and spindly bushes. On one end of the pond a deliberate pile of coral boulders decorated the waters edge. We planted a variety of tropical plants around this boulder barrier hoping to enhance its appearance.

We loved to wander our new pond and made regular trips to it. These visits became welcome learning experiences as we studied the various wildlife attached to it. We watched small schools of blue colored fish we knew to be blue tilapia and there were numerous minnows. We encountered turtle families thriving in our pond as well.

They were a familiar breed I'd seen many times in other ponds across our state. They were soft-shelled turtles that stayed under the water most of the time. They had long necks with snorkel shaped snouts and their shells were round like pancakes colored in an olive shade of green.

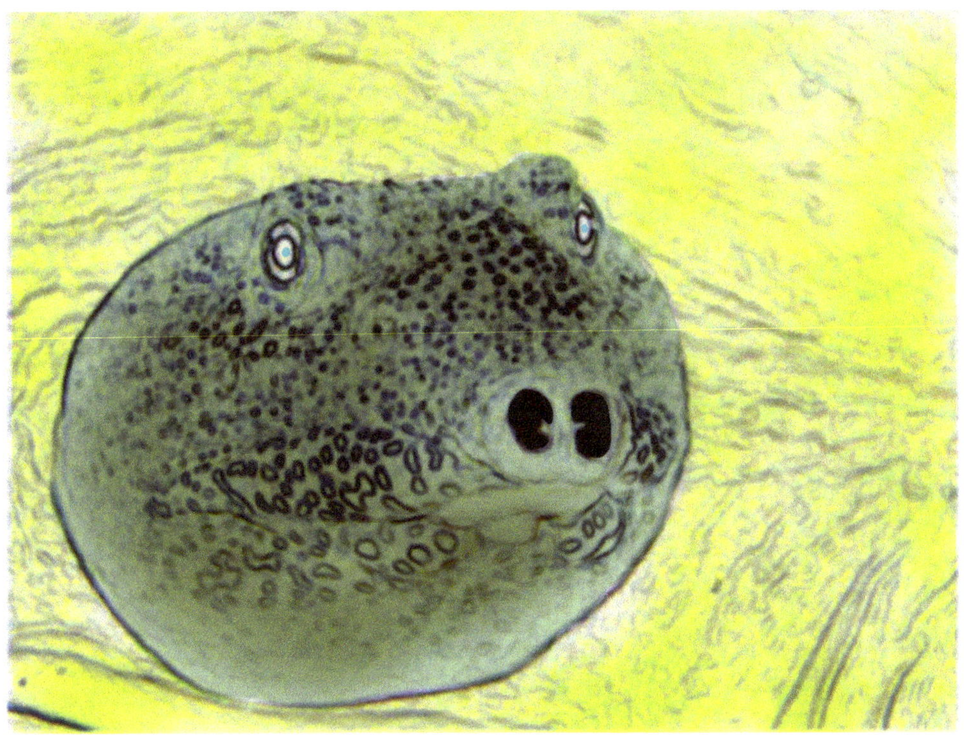

We would often take old bread and break it apart, tossing the pieces about the surface of the pond as it leaped with life. Minnows could be seen on the surface as they danced around these morsels that disappeared in a frenzy.

The beautiful hue of the blue tilapia broke the surface as they devoured their share of the goodies. Even turtle families, mothers, daddies and babies alike broke the surface to check out the flutter and share in the banquet presented. In no time the tidbits were gone, eaten by the residents of the pond.

We finally realized there wouldn't always be a steady supply of old bread and we took a special visit to a nearby tractor supply house that offered a generous variety of feed.

We checked out many aisles and discovered large bags of catfish floating feed. Knowing this would suit our pond dwelling friends, we made our purchase and headed back home.

There were other visitors to the pond as well. Our favorite was a tall bluish grey bird, standing perhaps forty inches high, with long stick like legs and a very hefty dark orange bill. His slender neck seemed almost as long as his legs. We called this handsome guy "Storky Bird". We enjoyed his visits and eventually learned he was a great blue heron.

Less frequently the white heron could be seen at the ponds edge. He looked much like the blue heron but of course he was covered in white feathers and sauntered by way of very dark colored legs.

Storky Bird frequently visited the pond to fish for dinner. He would wade around carefully and study the surface checking for shadows beneath. With a very quick dart of his beak, his task was finished, his meal complete.

Most every time we mowed the lawn, whole flocks of white ibis would arrive and follow each other through the yard pecking around for bugs. Smaller than the heron, these Florida birds were pure white with long bright orange beaks that curved downward. After a short stay they would all lift off together and fly to another yard. This was their routine throughout the summer while foraging for food.

The weather had changed, rain became scarce as a period of drought claimed our lands. As this pattern persisted our pond began to shrink and the water receded. This was worrisome indeed. However, this was the routine pattern that nature followed year after year, with some years dryer than others.

It seemed we had lost interest in our pond and neglected to visit it often. We didn't notice as much wildlife as we had seen a couple of months earlier.

You see, the animals could take care of themselves as they would adapt to these changes. For instance, the soft-shell turtles could bury themselves in the squishy mud at the bottom of the pond as their activity rested.

The fish and the minnows found refuge in the many grasses that filled the pond basin. This provided some safety and protection from predators and increasing warmth from the sun.

At long last the pond seemed to be drying up, as drought conditions persisted. Not much life appeared within it.

Storky Bird continued to make routine visits though. It must have been easy pickings for him now, fishing in such shallow water.

With summer underway the drought eased when a few rains brought welcome relief to the thirsty land.

These few rains multiplied over the following weeks increasing to one or two per day officially marking the beginning of our

rainy season. After a couple of very heavy downpours our pond waters rose a couple of feet above its original depth, a real blessing for the critters who might have survived this season's drought.

The additional chores of summer, including lawn maintenance, garden and plant care, pest control and many other things interfered with our day-to-day routine. We neglected to care for our pond community. After all, the pond survived before we ever came along and our concerns had lessened.

One early afternoon as I browsed the internet I noted a distinct tapping noise coming from our front room. I assumed it was the dogs making such noises. I glanced toward their sleeping area where I observed the two of them in a sound sleep.

"Did you hear that?" I asked my daughter Frieda. "It's not the dogs", I told her. More taps sounded. "Where is it coming from?"

I wanted to know. With a quick and alert twirl Frieda put her attention to the front door.

"It's coming from the front door", she announced, making her way there.

She pulled the taut curtains aside and peered through the windows of the double doors. At once she gave out with an unexpected laugh. "You have to see this", she bubbled.

I stepped up to the door not knowing what to expect, and peered out. There at the threshold of our entrance stood a very determined soft-shelled turtle, his partially webbed feet, and thick claws extended. He and he alone had used his claws to tap our door.

Not knowing what to do, Freida ran to pinch a piece of bread and offered it to the soft-shell.

He turned around abruptly and headed toward the pond at breakneck speed, leaving the pinch of bread behind.

We decided at that moment that our turtle friend had come to deliver a message. He wanted us to know that the pond community was alive and well and appreciated our gifts of food.

I determined to imagine that community beneath the water and how their story might be told. Perhaps they all got together in a sort of town meeting. The fish, the turtles, the minnows and others.

They might have discussed their critical needs. Maybe they were low on food supply.

Certainly they seemed desperate, having to send a spokes person to the great daunting door, hoping their message would be understood.

It's no surprise the capable Mr. Soft-Shell would be chosen for the task. He could survive out of water for the short stint, and he was quite swift on foot. To that end he had succeeded.

Whether the message was a desperate attempt to ask for food or not; It was the only thing we could imagine.

From that day to the present we have reinstated our policy to supply vittles to our friends in the pond and there have been no further visits from any of the pond inhabitants.

All is well!